ANYBODY CAN PLAY

By Jocelyn Stevenson
Illustrated by Tom Cooke

A SESAME STREET/READER'S DIGEST KIDS BOOK

Published by Reader's Digest Young Families, Inc.,
in cooperation with Children's Television Workshop

One rainy day on Sesame Street Bert couldn't think of anything to do.

He had already counted his paper clips and bottle caps and read his favorite pigeon book again.

Ernie came in out of the rain, soaking wet. "What a day!" he said.

"Hhhhhhhhhheeeeehhh," sighed Bert.

"Gee, Bert, old buddy. What's wrong?" Ernie asked.

"I just wish it weren't raining so I could go outside," said Bert.

"But, Bert, there are lots of things you can do inside," said Ernie. He ran into the bedroom and came back with a big box.

"Here's your bowling ball, Bert," he said. "You can count the holes in it!"

"Thanks, but no thanks," said Bert.

"Then what about wearing this funny mask?" asked Ernie.

"What's so funny about that?" said Bert glumly.

"I know what you can do, Bert. You can think about things—like penguins or tubas or elevators!"

"But that's what I've been doing, Ernie, and it's boring." Bert sighed again and sat down by the window. "I don't have anything to do but twiddle my thumbs."

"What's wrong with that, Bert?" asked Ernie. He put his thumbs in his ears and waggled his fingers. "And there are other nifty things you can do with your hands."

"I can't think of a thing," said Bert, putting his hands in his pockets.

"Then watch this,"
said Ernie, clapping his
hands above his head.
Bert clapped his hands
three times and stopped.
"Forget it," he said.

"But you haven't tried the good stuff
yet," cried Ernie. "What about this?"
He made a butterfly with his hands.

"Or this?" He rubbed his head with
one hand and patted his stomach with
the other. Bert just kept his hands in
his pockets.

"There are games we can play
with other parts of the body, Bert.
Let's try arms!" Ernie said
cheerfully.

First he made big circles with
his arms.

"We can swim, Bert!" he said,
and he "swam" around the room.

"I don't know how to swim,"
said Bert.

"Come on, Bert, old buddy,
try this!" Ernie touched his
elbows together.

"Or this!" He flapped
his arms like a chicken.

"Or this!" He clasped
his hands over his head
like a champion.

"That's no fun," said Bert.
"I wish I could go outside."

"It's still raining, Bert," said Ernie. "So let's do legs." Ernie hopped and skipped. Then he walked like a pigeon. Bert just watched.

"Hey, Bert," Ernie said. "Let's march."

Bert stood up and looked down at his legs. Slowly, little by little, he started to march with Ernie. First he marched with very tiny steps. Then he lifted his knees higher and higher. The more Bert marched, the more he liked it.

"Now let's do feet!" said Ernie, taking off his
sneakers and wiggling his toes. Bert took off his
saddle shoes and wiggled his toes, too.

Then Ernie grabbed a crayon with his toes and drew a picture. So did Bert.

"Now let's use our heads," said Ernie.
Ernie and Bert shook their heads back and forth.
Then they nodded their heads up and down.

Ernie looked up, up, up.
Bert looked down, down, down.

They rolled their heads in circles.

Then they stopped to think. "What are you
thinking about, Bert?" asked Ernie.
"I'm thinking about what to do next," said Bert.
"Let's do shoulders!" Bert lifted up his shoulders until
they almost touched his ears. Ernie put his shoulders
down.

Ernie put his shoulders forward.
Bert put his shoulders back.

"That's keen!" Bert said, and he began to walk
around the room moving his shoulders backward and
forward. "It's like marching with your shoulders!"

"Hey, Bert," said Ernie, "it's time for ribs. Put your hands on your sides and feel your ribs go in and out when you breathe."

"You're right!" Bert cried. "That's more fun than a flock of pigeons. What else can I do with my ribs?"

"You can count them," said Ernie.

So Bert counted his ribs. "What else, Ernie? What else are ribs for?" he asked.

"Well, Bert, old buddy," Ernie said.
"Ribs can be...TICKLED!"
And he tickled Bert's ribs until
Bert couldn't help laughing.

"What's next?" gasped Bert.
"We can do backs," Ernie said.
"What in the world can I do
with my back, Ernie?" Bert asked.

"I don't know, Bert. I'll rest while
you give it a try."
So Bert bent his back and then
he touched his toes.

He leaned to one side and
then to the other.

Then he started to twist from side
to side. "Come on, Ernie," he said,
"don't just sit there. Let's do the twist!"

"Hot dog! Let's do the whole body now, Ernie," said Bert. "Look! I can be a bird . . .

or an elephant . . .

or a frog . . .

or a snake! This is really
fun, Ernie!"
But Ernie was too tired
to play anymore.

Bert began leaping around the room,
dancing and turning somersaults.
Ernie looked out the window.

"Hey, Bert," he said. "Guess what.
It's stopped raining. Now we can go
outside!"

"Not now, Ernie," said Bert. "I still
have to do my wrists."

Ernie went outside and sat on the stoop in the sun.
"I know something else that my body can do," he
said. "It's called resting."
And he fell fast asleep.

This
PJ BOOK
belongs to

PJ Library®

JEWISH BEDTIME STORIES and SONGS

CHIK CHAK SHABBAT

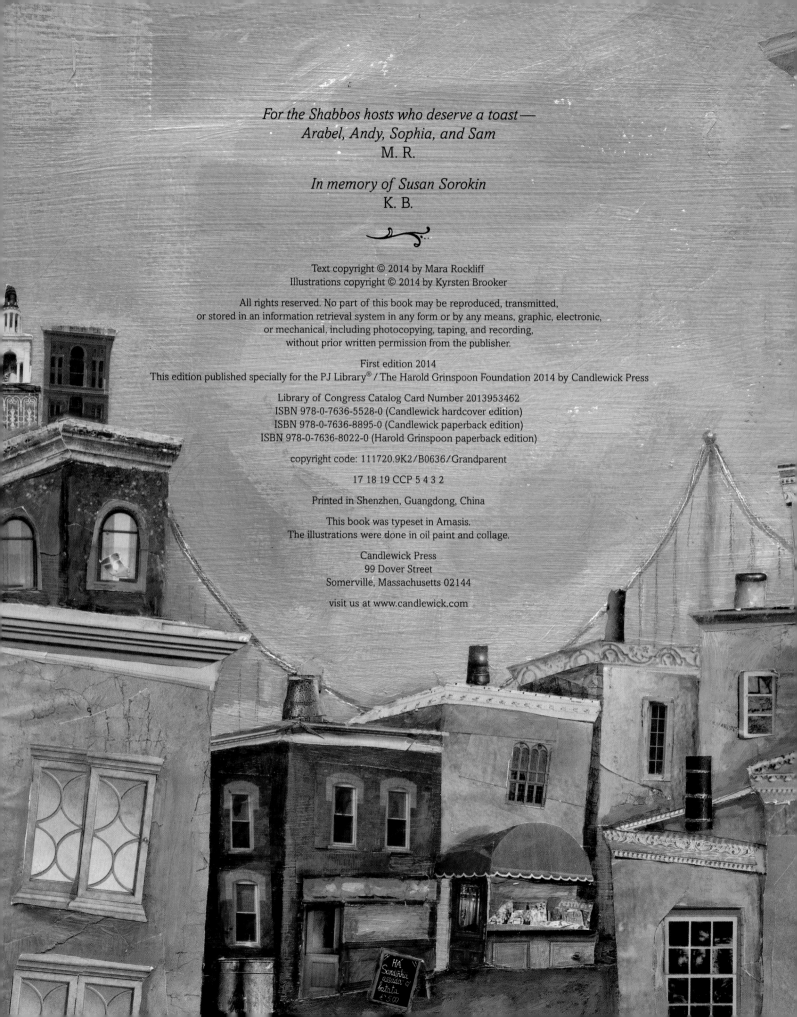

For the Shabbos hosts who deserve a toast—
Arabel, Andy, Sophia, and Sam
M. R.

In memory of Susan Sorokin
K. B.

Text copyright © 2014 by Mara Rockliff
Illustrations copyright © 2014 by Kyrsten Brooker

First edition 2014
This edition published specially for the PJ Library® / The Harold Grinspoon Foundation 2014 by Candlewick Press

Library of Congress Catalog Card Number 2013953462
ISBN 978-0-7636-5528-0 (Candlewick hardcover edition)
ISBN 978-0-7636-8895-0 (Candlewick paperback edition)
ISBN 978-0-7636-8022-0 (Harold Grinspoon paperback edition)

copyright code: 111720.9K2/B0636/Grandparent

17 18 19 CCP 5 4 3 2

Printed in Shenzhen, Guangdong, China

This book was typeset in Amasis.
The illustrations were done in oil paint and collage.

Candlewick Press
99 Dover Street
Somerville, Massachusetts 02144

visit us at www.candlewick.com

CHIK CHAK SHABBAT

Mara Rockliff   illustrated by Kyrsten Brooker

CANDLEWICK PRESS

Every Saturday, a wonderful smell wafted from apartment 5-A.

It curled into 4-D, tickling Tommy Santiago's nose as he played his tuba.

It slipped into 3-C, tempting Signora Bellagalli as she bustled around, dusting her teacups.

It crept under the door
of 2-B, tantalizing
Mr. Moon as he sat
typing his new
romance novel.

Even the Omar family
on the first floor caught
a whiff. They sniffed
the air and smiled.

At last, the door to 5-A flew open. Out stepped Goldie Simcha, her face shining like a silver spoon.

"Come in! Come in!
It's *cholent* time!"

As her neighbors took their places at her table,
Goldie ladled steaming stew into their bowls.

While they ate, they argued about what made
Goldie's *cholent* so delicious.

Signora Bellagalli cried,
"It's the tomatoes!"

"Or the barley?" offered Mr. Moon.

Little Lali Omar piped up, "The potatoes!"

And the Santiagos all agreed it had to be the beans.

But Goldie shook her head.

"When I was a girl," she said, "I always helped my grandmother get ready for Shabbat. All Friday afternoon, we rushed around:

cutting up vegetables,

sweeping the floor,

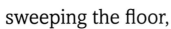

dressing the table in its best lace tablecloth.

Busy-busy, hurry-hurry, do it right away, *chik chak*!

But when the sun went down, my grandma lit the candles and Shabbat began."

"For one whole night and day, we put aside the things
that kept us busy all week long.

While the *cholent* bubbled slowly on the stove, we spent time in a special way—together."

"I don't celebrate Shabbat exactly as my grandma did," said Goldie. "But every Friday afternoon, I put a pot of *cholent* on the stove to bubble through the night and day. And when it's done at last, it has a special taste that isn't beans or barley, or tomatoes or potatoes. For me, the taste of *cholent* is . . . Shabbat."

And all her neighbors raised their spoons and said, "Shabbat!"

One Saturday, however, something wasn't right.

Tommy's tuba played nothing but sour notes.

Signora Bellagalli's nicest teacup tumbled off the shelf and smashed.

And Mr. Moon,
exasperated, hurled
the pages of his latest
romance novel right
across the room.

The Omars sniffed
and sniffed but couldn't
catch the faintest whiff.

At last, little Lali Omar climbed the stairs and knocked on Goldie's door.

Goldie answered, her face buried in a tissue. "Friday afternoon, I felt too sick to get the *cholent* on the stove," she said, and sniffled. "Now it's too late. You can't make *cholent* in a hurry, right away, *chik chak*!"

No *cholent* for Shabbat!

Tommy Santiago dropped his tuba
when he heard the news.

Signora Bellagalli's feather
duster flew into the air.

Mr. Moon got so mixed up,
he put a monster robot in his
romance novel and it squashed
the hero flat.

On the first floor, the Omars frowned.

"Poor Goldie," Mrs. Omar said.

"It just won't be Shabbat for her," Mr. Omar agreed.

Little Lali peered into the fridge. "Potato curry isn't the same thing as *cholent*," she said. "Still, it always cheers me up."

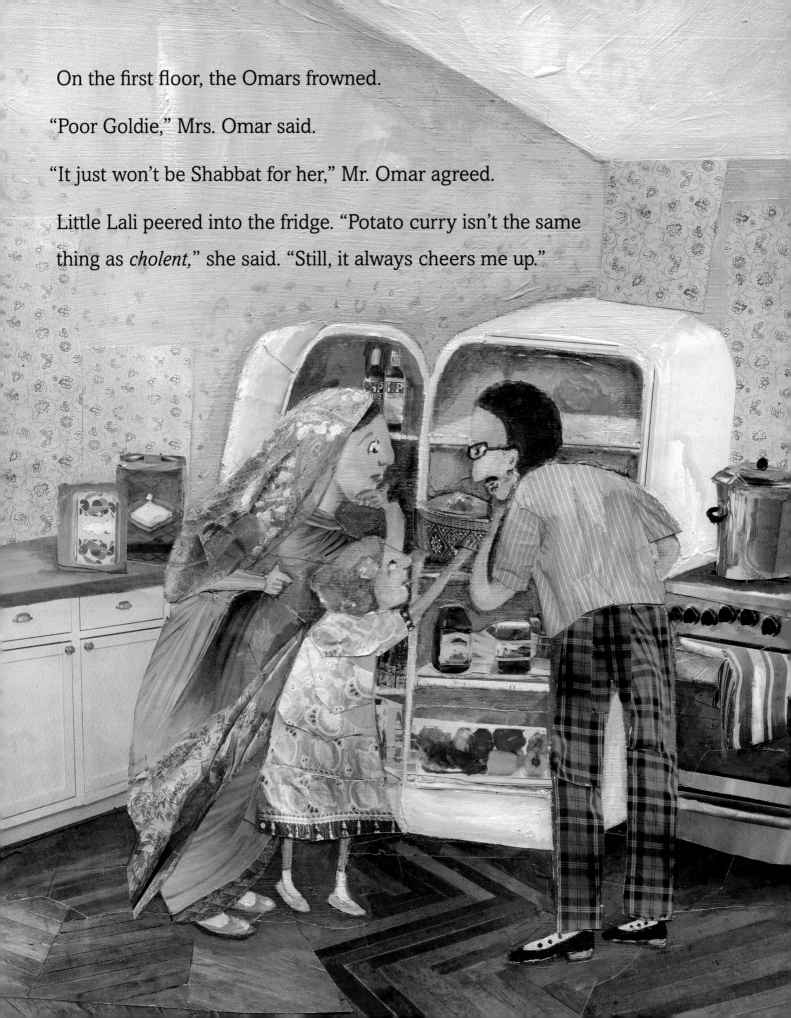

As the Omars climbed the stairs with their bowl of potato curry,
Mr. Moon came out of 2-B with a tray.

"Korean barley tea," he told them.

"Of course, it isn't *cholent,* but . . ."

Signora Bellagalli
squeezed out of 3-C.

"Tomato pizza," she
puffed. "It's not *cholent,*
but . . ."

Tommy Santiago held
the door of 4-D open
for his mother.

"It's not *cholent,*"
she admitted cheerfully.
"But everyone likes
beans and rice."

Goldie opened the door for them. She blew her nose,
wiped her eyes, and smiled. "Come in! Come in!"

Her neighbors took their places at her table, and they filled their plates.

"We didn't have time to make anything special," Signora Bellagalli apologized. "We had to hurry-hurry, bring it right away, *chik chak*! But . . ."

"But here we are," said little Lali Omar.
"Together."

Goldie took a bite of pizza. A nibble of
curry. A mouthful of beans and rice.
She sipped her barley tea.

Then she looked around the table, her face shining like a silver spoon, and said, "I think it tastes exactly like Shabbat."

CHOLENT

Goldie's grandmother cooked cholent *with a special cut of meat called flanken,
but Goldie's recipe is vegetarian. Either way is good. Just be sure to leave plenty of time,
because there is one way you can't cook* cholent: *in a hurry, right away,* chik chak!

INGREDIENTS

Olive oil

2 large onions, chopped

28-ounce can diced tomatoes

1 cup barley

4 or 5 potatoes, peeled and cut into chunks

1½ cups dried beans (any kind—Goldie likes to mix garbanzo, white, and pinto beans)

2 carrots, peeled and cut into chunks

Water or vegetable broth

Salt and pepper

DIRECTIONS

1. Heat a big pot on the stove, then pour a little oil in it.

2. When the oil is hot, add the onions and stir until they're fried.

3. Add the tomatoes, barley, potatoes, beans, and carrots.

4. Add enough water or broth to make it stew.

5. Add salt, pepper, and any other flavorings you like.*

6. Bring the stew to a boil, then turn the heat down very low so it simmers.

7. Cook for a long time. All day is good. All night is even better.

8. *B'tayavon!* Eat and enjoy!

*Goldie throws in a couple of bay leaves, a few good squirts of ketchup, and a lot of smoked paprika. You could also try garlic powder, cumin, onion soup mix, or even veggie sausages.

Another fun thing to do is (gently) drop in whole eggs in their shells and let them cook. When the *cholent* is ready, remove the eggs with a slotted spoon and let them cool. Then peel the shells and you'll have *cholent*-flavored hard-boiled eggs!

MARA ROCKLIFF is the author of many books for children, including *The Grudge Keeper* and *Me and Momma and Big John,* a Charlotte Zolotow Honor Book and Golden Kite Award Winner. She lives in eastern Pennsylvania with her family. Visit her online at www.mararockliff.com.

KYRSTEN BROOKER has illustrated many award-winning books for children, including *The Honeybee Man,* a Bank Street College Best Children's Book of the Year, and *Precious and the Boo Hag,* an American Library Association Notable Children's Book, a *School Library Journal* Best Book of the Year, and a Charlotte Zolotow Honor Book. Kyrsten Brooker lives in Alberta, Canada, with her family.